NANCY WARREN

A Diamond Choker For Christmas

A TONI DIAMOND MYSTERY

ISBN: ebook 978-1-928145-28-8

ISBN: print 978-1-928145-99-8

Cover Design by Stunning Book Covers

Ambleside Publishing

INTRODUCTION

Will this Holiday Open House be her Last?

Toni Diamond's mom, Linda, has joined a marketing success group to help her achieve amazing results as a Lady Bianca Cosmetics sales consultant. Unfortunately, her latest plan to manifest success is to borrow a priceless necklace to wear to her annual Christmas party in her mobile home. Toni's worried somebody may try to steal the valuable jewels — but the truth is much deadlier. The Diamond family's holiday cheer may turn into holiday fear!

A DIAMOND CHOKER FOR CHRISTMAS

CHAPTER 1

*T*oni Diamond heard the ping signaling a text message. As though the signal had an echo, her daughter Tiffany received a text at the same time.

They glanced at each other across the kitchen. Toni was in the midst of pouring her second cup of Monday morning coffee. Tiff was munching granola at the breakfast bar. They both checked their phones. No surprise, both texts were from Linda, Toni's mother: *Remember my beautiful girls, what we imagine happens! Imagine success today!*

"She went to her positive thinking meet-up group last night, didn't she?" Tiffany asked.

At seventeen, Tiff was growing into a real beauty, though she still didn't embrace Lady Bianca cosmetics the way Toni hoped she would. Since Toni and her mom made their living as independent consultants for Lady Bianca Cosmetics, she'd hoped to bring Tiffany into the family business. So far, her daughter would barely use a swipe of lip-gloss, but she was young yet.

"Probably."

1

"She's addicted," Tiffany said. She flipped back through the string of texts she and Toni received several times a day. "She's addicted to positive thinking."

"Well, it's harmless," Toni replied.

"It's the crack of self-help," Tiffany maintained.

Another text alert rang out for both of them.

Girls, fantastic idea for Christmas Party. I'm going to manifest diamonds. We create our reality.

"Seriously, Mom, Grandma's lost the program."

Linda Plotnik hosted a Christmas party every year at her mobile home park and invited all her neighbors, customers, potential customers, and of course, her daughter and granddaughter. Her party was this Saturday, four days away.

"What did she mean about manifesting diamonds?" Toni asked, feeling the first qualm of uneasiness about her mother for the day. And she'd been up all of thirty-five minutes.

"With Grandma? Who knows?" Tiffany went back to munching her fair-trade granola and Toni took another fortifying sip of coffee. "By the way, I can't go to Grandma's Christmas party this year. I've got to work on my college entrance papers. After all, you're the one who wants me to go to college."

"Nice try, sweet pea. You'd no more break Grandma's heart than I'd go out of the house without lipstick."

Tiffany took her now empty bowl to the dishwasher. "Thursday is the holiday party for the kids at the hospital."

"And you're volunteering?" Tiffany helped out a couple of times a week. She said it was to strengthen her college applications, but Toni could see how much she enjoyed helping out with sick kids. "Yes. Then Becca wants me to sleep over at her place Thursday night. We'll be studying late."

Tiffany was one of the few kids who, if she told her mother she was going to a sleepover in order to study, was going to a sleepover in order to study. Coming from the Diamond/Plotnik gene pool, this girl was a miracle.

Half an hour later, Tiff had left for school and Toni was showered, dressed and putting the final touches on her makeup. After years of practice, she had her routine down to fifteen minutes, not including cleansing and moisturizing. It was while she was darkening her brows with Lady Bianca's Cocoa Bean eyebrow pencil that she saw her own eyes widen in the mirror.

What was her mom always saying? Manifest what you want to appear. How was she planning to manifest real diamonds? That was the part of the text that had Toni blinking at her own startled reflection. Did her mother think she could mine gems through positive thinking?

The following afternoon, she had her answer when Linda showed up at their door.

"Well, girls, what do you think?"

Toni could not find the words. Linda had one of her most opulent hairpieces on, and she looked like a cross between Marie Antoinette and a Vegas showgirl. Her false eyelashes glittered, her makeup was on the brighter side of flashy, and her figure-hugging white and silver pantsuit bared a lot of cleavage. But what had Toni's eyes bugging out of her head was the flash and sparkle that encircled her neck. The necklace was diamond and sapphire; big, gorgeously cut stones that glittered with suppressed fire. Toni might not be a gemologist, but she could tell fake from real when it came to diamonds.

Those were not fake.

Her answer to the question came suddenly as she pulled her mother inside the house. "That should be locked up."

"Locked up?" Linda asked, looking bewildered.

"She means the necklace should be locked up, Grandma, not you," Tiffany said from behind Toni, though, in fact, she wasn't so sure that was what she'd meant.

"Where did you get the bling, Grandma? Did you knock over the jeweler's at the mall?"

Instead of looking appalled that her granddaughter considered her capable of a jewel heist, Linda appeared delighted at the idea. "Wouldn't it be exciting? To have all that gorgeous jewelry and all you had to do was reach in and grab it and stuff it in a velvet bag? Not even to consider your credit card limit for a second?"

"And then do five to ten in jail once you got caught," Toni put in.

"Oh, you're such a spoilsport. It was fun to imagine for a moment. I always thought being a cat burglar would be so exciting. If I wasn't so bad at climbing ropes." She glanced down at her impressive chest. "I think it's being so well endowed. Throws off the center of gravity."

"Where did you get the necklace, Mom?"

"I borrowed it."

"Borrowed it?"

"Yes. For my Christmas party. You know how at the Oscars Harry Winston always loans out the most fabulous pieces for the Hollywood stars to wear? That's where I got the idea."

"You went to Harry Winston?" Toni felt faint.

"Of course not. I went to a local jeweler. Lone Star Gems and Jewels."

However, Linda wasn't a Hollywood star and their local jeweler wasn't going to get a lot of business from a Christmas party in a mobile home park populated mainly by seniors.

"And they let you borrow it?"

"Of course. Bert Green, he's the owner of Lone Star Jewels, he's in my Circle of Success meet-up group." Linda walked to the hall mirror and turned to one side and then the other. "Just look at the fire in those stones. You simply can't duplicate the look of a real diamond."

"What's it worth, Grandma?"

"This piece retails for more than a hundred thousand dollars, but Bert's promised me a very nice discount when I buy it."

"A nice discount." Toni rarely drank alcohol during the week, but she was starting to feel the need for a stiff drink.

"That's right." Linda turned to Tiffany. "You noticed I said *when*. Very important for success that we speak of our dreams and, even more vital, believe in them as though they've already happened. I said I wanted a fabulous diamond-and-jewel necklace to wear at my party, and here I am wearing it. Positive thinking is amazingly powerful."

"How did you pull it off, Mom?" Toni was a big believer in the power of positive thinking, too, but Linda seemed to be taking the concept a little far.

"They put a lien on my home."

"A lien?" Tiffany asked.

"Yes, it means I signed a paper saying that if anything happens to the necklace, they can take my mobile home. Of course, nothing's going to happen. It was just a formality."

"You put up your house as collateral for a diamond necklace?"

"I'm only borrowing it, honey."

"But what if something happens? You lose it, or it accidentally gets caught in the garbage disposal?"

"My garbage disposal is broken, so that's never going to happen. Besides, if anything awful happened, I'd move in here. You've got plenty of room. Gosh, I can't believe we've never thought of that before. It would be like a girls' slumber party every night."

Scotch. There must be a bottle of scotch somewhere in the house.

"Anyway, we're all friends at the group and we all believe in each other. At first, Bert wasn't sure about lending the necklace at all because it's so valuable, but Henry Castillo, he's the lawyer in our success circle, he stepped up and said he'd take on the risk. He's the one who drew up the paperwork. So then everyone was happy."

"The party's not for four more days. Where are you going to keep the necklace?"

Linda ran her fingers over the gems. "In a very secret hiding place."

Toni groaned. "Mo-ther, if it's at the bottom of the trash can in the bathroom, please just don't."

Linda's eyes opened so wide one of the sparkle tips snapped off her fake eyelashes. "How did you know? I read that idea years ago and always thought it was the perfect place to hide something important because no thief would ever look there."

"I know because you hid the grocery money there when I was a kid and then threw it out with the trash."

Linda's hand flew to her open mouth. "Oh, my gosh, I did. But we got it back."

"Only because you remembered before the trash got collected. We spent hours going through the household garbage before we unearthed it."

"Well, I'll find a better hiding place this time."

"Why don't you get the store to hang onto it until the day of the party? They have a safe and a security system."

"Sweetie, I think it's important for my self-development to wear this fabulous necklace. It's a constant reminder to myself that I am worth it!"

When her mom got stubborn, she pursed her lips so that with her red lipstick the shape was very much like a stop sign. Toni knew there was no point arguing any longer. All she could do at this point was hope that nothing happened to that expensive bit of bling. And maybe talk to an architect about building a mother-in-law cottage in her back yard.

"Anyway, I want to wear it to my Circle of Success meeting tonight."

CHAPTER 2

*T*iffany and her mother exchanged glances. Toni could not find words to adequately express her feelings. And for Toni that was not a normal state of affairs. She'd discovered in herself a talent for sales that was remarkable enough that she was one of the top representatives for Lady Bianca cosmetics in all of the country. But she knew when she was facing a prospect who was a dud. There was a time to stop selling since she was wasting her time. Trying to sell her mother on the idea that the fabulous necklace should be locked up safely until her party was hopeless.

"Tell me more about this success group, Mama."

"Well, honey, I'd ask you to join it but we only allow one person from any industry. That way, there's no competition. The idea is that we all use each other's services as well as motivating and encouraging each other. But, let's see, we talk about sales techniques, and each week we start out by sharing our biggest success of the week. We all applaud and cheer each other on. William Young, he's a real estate investor and you would not believe how successful he's been. He started picking up foreclosures and now he's a multi-million-aire. I should introduce you to him. It would be good for you to diversify your portfolio."

Since her portfolio consisted of paying off her house and saving up for Tiffany's college fees, she didn't think Mr. Young would find her very interesting.

"I don't want you to think that we're all only interested in money, we absolutely make sure we give back. Katie Lewis, she's the caterer in the group, she volunteers for the Girl Guides. Henry Castillo is an amateur magician. He goes to hospitals and old folks' homes and entertains them with magic tricks. And I'm teaching step dancing to the other residents of Pecan Heights."

"You've been busy."

The jewels sparkled as she admired them once more in the hall mirror. "I'm having the time of my life."

"You want some coffee, Mama?"

Linda glanced at her glittery watch and shook her head. "I have to run. I've got to get to my Zumba class." Since discovering Zumba onboard a cruise the three women had taken, Linda had become a firm devotee of the aerobics and dance fusion classes.

When Linda left, Toni turned to her daughter. "What are we going to do?"

"She should have a bodyguard. Somebody big and armed and dangerous."

"I don't know anyone like that. But I do know a cop."

There were moments when having a friendly relationship with a Dallas detective was a real benefit. Toni felt that this was one of those times. She called Luke Marciano on his cellphone.

"Marciano," he snarled the name. Since he obviously knew it was her calling, he was snarling because he was busy, because one of his colleagues could overhear him, or because he was in a bad mood.

"Hi, honey. Bad day?" she asked.

"No worse than usual. Busy."

Okay, she could take a broad hint. "Why don't you call me back when you're not so busy."

"Will it be good news?"

"Call me back and find out." They saw each other when they could, but between his work schedule, her work schedule, and Tiffany's schedule, they didn't connect as often as they'd like. She thought the arrangement suited both of them. For now.

"No, it's okay, I've got five."

"Well, it's kind of a good news, bad news situation."

"Good news first." As a detective, he worked with bad news all day. She understood that his relationship with her was one of the bright spots in his life, even if she did have an unfortunate habit of finding trouble.

"Tiffany's sleeping over at her friend's on Thursday."

"Does that mean her mom's available for a sleepover too?" When he wasn't snarling, he had the sexiest voice.

"It does."

"I'll pencil you in." There was a moment's silence, and then he said. "Okay, what's the bad news?"

"It's my mother."

"What's she done this time?"

"Luke, she's borrowed a fabulously expensive necklace to wear to her Christmas party this Saturday."

"Who'd she borrow it from?"

"A jewelry store. They put a lien on her house before they'd lend it to her."

Luke was smart and intuitive, which made him a great detective. Also, he knew Linda, so she didn't have to explain all the ways this was a terrible idea. "Where is it now?"

"Around her neck. If I had to guess, I'd say she's wearing it to Zumba class, the grocery store, her sales calls, all around her mobile home park."

"What's it worth?"

"A hundred grand."

In his silence, she could hear the curse words he didn't voice.

"Want me to talk to her?"

"It won't do any good. She's determined that wearing real jewels will manifest success in her life."

"More likely to get her robbed."

"That's my biggest fear. If she loses her home, you know where she's going, don't you?"

He chuckled. "Better start cleaning up your spare room."

She did not join in his amusement. "You can come as my date if you want. It's her annual Christmas open house."

"I know. I got the e-vite."

"How did she get your email address?" Linda hadn't mentioned that she was inviting Luke to her party. Toni wasn't surprised. Linda made no secret of the fact that she thought Luke would make an excellent son-in-law.

"Maybe she manifested it," he said drily.

She didn't figure either of them needed detective skills to work out that Linda had sneaked into Toni's office and taken Luke's email from her computer. "Sorry. Please don't feel like you have to come."

"I'll try to drop by." She knew he was busy on the weekends. If he wasn't working, he restored antique cars and trucks as a hobby, played sports, and caught up on his household chores.

If Linda insisted on wearing a valuable necklace, she thought having a cop around would be as good as hiring a security guard. "I'd appreciate it."

TONI HAD JUST FINISHED her weekly sales report and, to her satisfaction, her team's sales were rocking, when her mother called. "Honey, I need your help with the lights." Something about the tone behind those words filled Toni with dread.

"What lights, Mama?"

"Why, the Christmas lights, of course."

"I thought the caretaker put up the lights. He's done it every other year." Jim Tucker had been the caretaker of Pecan Heights Mobile Home Park for as long as Toni could remember. He was long and lean, with pale blue eyes in a darkly tanned face. He didn't say much, and she could never recall him either cracking a joke or laughing at one. But Jim kept the grounds clean, made sure the trash was always picked up on time, and if a resident needed their windows cleaned or some extra chores done around the house, Jim was always available if the person paid him in cash.

One of his responsibilities was the decorating of the park grounds for the holidays. He strung the clubhouse with white twinkle lights and in the main square of the mobile home park, he put up the same wooden Santa waving from a wooden sleigh and surrounded by wooden reindeer that had decorated the park for the last dozen or so holidays.

On top of that, residents were invited to decorate their own homes in whichever way pleased. Somewhere along the way a competitive spirit overtook the residents of Pecan Heights and every year the holiday splendor exploded with so many colorful lights, dazzling displays and neon candy canes that Toni always make sure she had her sunglasses in her bag if she went to visit her mother during the last part of December. Linda had put up most of her decorations, with Jim Tucker's help, at the beginning of December.

"I bought a few more strands of lights. I learned so much from my master sales techniques group. I even want my holiday decorations to help celebrate my success. I was just up on the roof but it's a bit windy and I don't think I can manage to put up all the lights by myself."

"Roof?" Toni was already reaching for her car keys. "Mama, I'll be right there. Don't even think about going up on that roof again without me."

Naturally, Toni had a lot of work to do, and naturally, she had not scheduled in time to travel out to her mom's place and climb up on the roof.

Swiftly, she changed her cream wool skirt and cranberry silk blouse for a pair of jeans, sneakers and an old shirt she wore for doing dirty chores. She reminded herself as she drove that she was practicing prevention. She'd lose a lot more time from work if her mom ended up in the hospital with a broken leg from falling off her own roof.

When she pulled up in front of her mother's home, she blinked. Toni loved sparkle, glitter and pizazz, but Linda had taken glitz to a whole new level. it looked as though her mother had driven to Vegas and stolen every light bulb and scrap of neon in the city and stuck it all on her property.

Her mother was currently stringing white and green and red lights around the neck of the Virgin Mary.

She wore tight jeans, a pair of blue and silver cowboy boots, enough platinum curls for three showgirls, and a denim shirt with diamond snaps. The shirt was tight enough to reveal that even in her late fifties, Linda Plotnik had kept her trim waist and curvy figure. It was also open at the neck to display the diamond and sapphire necklace in all its glory.

She waved. "Honey, you're just in time. You can put the ruby and diamond belt on the first wise man."

Toni stepped forward across the white pebbles, her sneakers scrunching as she grew closer. "Do you really think the Virgin Mary would be decked out in all those jewels? I mean, if she had all that bling, wouldn't she have pawned something so she could give birth maybe in a nice hotel or a house instead of a manger?"

Her mother laughed. "Of course she would, silly. The wise men brought her jewels as gifts. Think about it. They brought gold and frankincense and myrrh for the baby. I like to think they also had some gifts for the new mother. And nobody bothered to write it down."

"I guess it's possible."

"In my version it is. So I need you to help me haul the manger scene up onto the roof."

Toni would have suggested leaving the scene somewhere in the yard but it was crammed full of snowmen, life-sized jolly-looking Santas with sparkling gifts and dazzling reindeer. Icicles hung from all around the roof of the mobile home, and lights twinkled from every window and door-frame, every inch of railing and the roofline.

It was clear from the number of electrical leads that every one of those reindeer, Santas, and candy canes lit up when plugged in. She had her suspicions that at least some of them flashed on and off, probably to a sprightly Christmas tune.

"The diamond halos are a nice touch," she said.

She eyed the roof. She did not relish the thought of climbing up there with the nativity scene. "Did you think of asking Jim Tucker to put the nativity scene up on the roof?" she asked, shading her eyes and gazing up and down the street hopefully. Her eye was snagged by the neighbor's house across the street, where the front yard was filled by a giant teddy bear wearing an actual Christmas sweater.

"Did Mrs. Schwartz knit that sweater herself?" It was dark green with giant red stars patterned on it.

"She did. She's so sly. She never mentioned a word about it to anyone. She said it took her all year to knit it."

At Teddy's feet were wrapped gifts, most of them huge, and decorated with elaborate bows. While the two women watched, a tiny man who looked more elf than human came out of the house. He was carrying a bundle of red and green wool.

"Hi, Mr. Schwartz," Toni called out.

"Ah, Toni, how are you? Linda, your decorations look very nice."

While they watched, he retrieved a stepladder from behind his mobile home, set it up and then climbed the steps. He leaned out precariously to wrap a scarf around Teddy's neck. The scarf must have been fifty feet long and flapped roguishly in the breeze, slapping tiny Mr. Schwartz as he attempted to lasso the bear's head.

Mrs. Schwartz came bustling out. She waved to Toni and Linda, then stood at the foot of the ladder supervising her husband. She was as large as he was tiny and she waved her arms like a conductor as she directed him. "No, no, Archie, I want the scarf looped more in the front."

"Phylis, I'm gonna fall off the darn ladder if I lean any more."

"I spent every evening for a year working on that sweater and the hat and the scarf. Don't tell me you can't spend five minutes on a ladder."

Mr. Schwartz grumbled back, "In five minutes I could fall off this ladder and break my neck."

As Mrs. Schwartz was about to reply, a porch door banged from the mobile home right next door to Linda. A plus-sized woman wearing a purple velour tracksuit stomped down the three steps covered with artificial grass and plastic daisies to where a yellow muscle car sat in the driveway. "Morning, Esther!" Linda called, waving to her neighbor.

The woman nodded her head though her sour expression didn't change. She had a bad perm and the brassy blond curls did not suit her reddened complexion. She started up the car with a roar and then reversed out of her driveway and raced down Pecan Lane, slamming her brakes just before she hit the speed bump with the ease of long practice.

"Why did you wave to her?" Toni asked. "Isn't she the woman who tried to sue you?"

"She sued the Moores on the other side over a fence. She tried to get me thrown out of Pecan Heights for running a business out of my home." Linda shrugged. "What am I going to do? She's my neighbor. Anyway, I feel kind of sorry for her. No one in the park likes her very much because she's so mean and she's always trying to make a buck suing people. And," another charming shrug, "everyone likes me. It is technically against our bylaws for anyone to run a business out of their home here in Pecan Heights, but when our board met, I simply explained that I run most of my business elsewhere. I mean, I go to my clients' houses for makeup parties and to give them makeovers. I only keep my stock in my spare bedroom. Naturally, the board agreed with me and adjusted the bylaws. Esther Kilpatrick was furious."

"Why would she even care? It's not like you have a lot of people coming over and parking all over the street and making noise or anything." Well, except for the party she had ever year at Christmas time.

Mrs. Schwartz, who had crossed the street in order to supervise the correct jaunty angle for the knitted cap that her husband was placing on Teddy's head, said, "It's because she wants that her daughter should move into the park. That son-in-law is no good and she wants to keep an eye on him if you ask me. But our park is full. If she could get Linda thrown out, she could have her daughter living next door. Trouble is, nobody likes her daughter either and that son-in-law is a hooligan. Esther's daughter is exactly like her mother. They sue people to make money. One in the park is bad enough, who wants two of them?"

"Oh, well," Linda said, "I always say, let bygones be bygones."

"What about when you have your party? Will she make trouble?"

Linda shook her head. "I always invite her to the party. I figure that way she has nothing to complain about."

Mrs. Schwartz took her eyes off her husband for a moment and said, "If you ask me, Esther's plain jealous of you." She turned to Toni. "Your mother is a very attractive woman and if she ever wanted to get married there are plenty of older gentleman in the park who would be happy to have her." Then she glanced back and raised her voice. "No, Archie, the pom-pom is falling over his nose. I don't want Teddy's pom-pom hanging over his face, it's supposed to rest against his ear."

Mr. Schwartz fought the scarf that was smacking him and pushed the pom-pom toward the ear, but the breeze knocked it back over the bear's nose. "If I'm doing such a terrible job, maybe you'd like to come over here and get on this ladder and do it yourself."

Mrs. Schwartz threw her hands in the air. "I don't know why I bother." She stomped back across the road and began a spirited argument with her husband while the pom-pom bobbed gently up and down.

CHAPTER 3

*T*oni managed to get the nativity scene on top of her mother's roof with the help of Mr. Schwartz who, she thought, was glad to get away from Mrs. Schwartz for a few minutes. He brought his ladder and a willing pair of hands. He and Toni hauled the nativity scene onto the top of the roof, where he secured it. "It's not going to fall down, is it?" Toni asked. "That Esther Kilpatrick will probably sue my mother if it falls."

"No promises, but I don't think so."

Toni broke a nail but other than that climbed back off the roof unharmed.

Mr. Schwartz declined an offer of iced tea and headed back to his own home on the other side of the street. As he left, Linda called, "Don't forget to come to my party on Saturday."

"Wouldn't miss it," he yelled back.

When Toni entered her mother's mobile home she discovered that Linda had been busy decorating inside as well as out. A particularly glitzy Madonna and Child held pride of place on top of the mantel of Linda's electric fireplace. "I don't remember seeing this before."

"My friend Maria Lopez gave it to me. She lives in the park too but she's going home to Mexico for Christmas, and when she saw how much I love glitter and glamour, she brought over her own Madonna. It's funny how the Latino culture shares my belief that Mother Mary was a very glamorous woman." She glanced at her daughter. "Do you think I could be part Mexican?"

"Anything's possible."

Naturally, Linda had draped glamorous Madonna with even more crystals and beads and diamonds. In fact, she'd draped lights and sparkles everywhere. One corner of the living/dining area held a white flocked Christmas tree and instead of her usual ornaments, she had decorated the tree entirely with Lady Bianca Holiday Glitter sample packs. Toni was duly impressed. "Mom, that's a great idea. What a fun way to market our products."

Linda beamed with pride. "I knew you'd like it. I was saving the tree as a surprise. What I'm going to do, on Saturday, is give everybody one of the sample packs with an offer for a free makeover and my contact information." She patted her neck where the diamond and sapphire necklace settled as though it belonged there. "Every sample, every makeover, every referral, gets me one step closer to manifesting this necklace."

Toni might worry about her mother wearing such an expensive piece of jewelry everywhere she went, but she couldn't fault her logic. "Absolutely! You're closer to owning that necklace with every minute you put into your business. I'll bring some of my extra stock, too, in case you run out."

"Aww, honey, that is so sweet of you."

Linda had strung her Christmas cards on lines of glittery twine, and while her mother was in the kitchen pouring the drinks, Toni idly began to go through them. Then she came to one and smiled. "Mom, you got a Christmas card from Roy, the guy you met on the cruise."

When Linda came in carrying two glasses of iced tea, she was blushing a little. "I know. We've been emailing almost every day."

"Wow. Really? Doesn't he live in the Midwest somewhere?"

"He does. He sells car parts in Omaha. I think he was having a rough patch at work and I was able to send him some motivational quotes and ideas of books on positive thinking. It's amazing how you can change your life just by changing your thoughts."

"It sure is, Mama. Also how well you can get to know someone on email. And how strange it is that you didn't tell me or Tiffany."

They settled on the couch and Toni noticed a photograph of herself and Tiffany and Linda that had been taken on board the cruise ship they had taken in the fall. Beside it was a second photograph that she didn't recall seeing before. It showed Linda and Roy standing together and smiling at the camera.

He might be a little younger than her mom but it was clear that he was quite smitten with her. "Oh, well," Linda said, following her gaze. "He is a few years younger than me, and so far we're just pen pals."

Since she was here anyway, and her mother was one of her sales associates, Toni decided to make lemonade out of lemons and have a business discussion with her mom. She pulled out her notebook computer and opened a file. "How are you doing with your Christmas bookings?"

Linda beamed. "I'm doing great, honey. I can't believe how much a clear and visible target, like this necklace, helps a girl to focus on her goals. I booked six home parties and I'll be doing four home makeovers this week. I think one of the party hostesses would be a really good candidate to become a Lady Bianca rep." The goal of every rep was to sign up new reps and broaden her network. Lady Bianca sales associates earned money from their own product sales but also earned a percentage of every sale of every consultant they recruited. Toni's network was big enough that she made more of her income from her sales team than from her own sales, though she had a large customer base of her own.

"That's fantastic, Mom." There was a reason she rarely had one-on-one business meetings with her mother. There was no need. Linda was enthusiastic and a real go-getter.

"So, what time do you want Tiffany and me to arrive on Saturday? And what can we bring?" Normally, she helped Linda load up at Costco with cheese and crackers and snack foods and so on and helped set up the bar. But Linda shook her head. "I don't want you to do a thing. You and Tiffany are here as guests. I hired a caterer," she said with pride.

"You did?"

"I did. I'm a hard-working businesswoman and if I act successful, I will be successful."

"It's the caterer from your success circle, isn't it?"

"It sure is. Katie. I'm hiring her for my party and she's hosting one of the Christmas glitter parties at her house. That's how the success circle works."

"Okay. Makes sense."

"She's taking care of everything. She's renting the glasses, bringing all the beverages and the food. It's going to be so easy. I'll get to relax and mingle with my guests. I can't wait. I just love holiday parties."

As Toni was leaving, her daughter called. "Mom, I'm finished with my work at the hospital. It was fun. We had a party for the kids with pizza and a juggler and a magician. Everyone had a great time. But I'm wondering if you can pick me up."

"Aren't you going to Becca's tonight for a sleepover?"

"Yeah, but I want to change and pick up a book I forgot. Also, can I borrow the car? I'll bring it back in the morning."

"You going cruising for guys?"

Her daughter made a rude noise. "When are you going to realize I am nothing like you?"

"A mother has her dreams."

She didn't think Luke would mind coming to her place later if she was carless, so she agreed. As she pulled into the hospital lot later, she noticed a yellow muscle car. Since her ex-husband Dwayne had been car crazy, she knew the model. It was a 1970 Plymouth Roadrunner. Strange to see two in one day, as that was the same car her mom's next-door neighbor had been driving. While she watched idly, the passenger door opened and a tall, distinguished looking man got out. She caught a glimpse of silver hair. He wore jeans and a polo shirt but something about the way he carried himself suggested he was more at home in a suit.

Tiffany ran out of the side door a few minutes later and jumped into Toni's car. "Thanks, Mom. You're the best."

"Do you want dinner before you go, Tiff?"

Her daughter threw her a teasing glance. "Three's a crowd."

She refused to blush. She was a grown woman and if she carried on a discreet relationship with a cop who was also single, that was her business. Her one rule was that Luke was never allowed to sleep over when Tiffany was in the house, and she never slept at his place if her daughter was around. However, Tiff was perfectly well aware that Luke was the man in her mom's life.

"I don't know what you mean," she replied. "I plan to spend the evening knitting you a sweater exactly like the one that Mrs. Schwartz knit for a gigantic teddy bear in her front yard."

"Seriously?" her daughter laughed. "I can't wait to see it."

"Did I mention the bear lights up?"

"I should get my environmental club to do an intervention. I swear, the way those residents in Pecan Heights try to outdo each other, one of these days they'll blow the electric grid."

CHAPTER 4

*I*t was a typical December day in the Dallas suburbs the day of Linda's party, around sixty degrees and sunny. Since her mother had hired a caterer for the festivities, Toni was free to spend the morning doing anything she liked. She fixed her broken nail as best she could but still made an appointment with her manicurist to replace the nail. When her daughter rolled out of bed, she said, "I tell you what, Tiff. Why don't you and I go shopping this morning and I'll treat you to a manicure."

Her daughter, unlike every other seventeen-year-old girl Toni could think of, did not jump up and down with excitement. She glanced at her fingernails, which she had painted herself with black polish. "I'm not having little diamonds on my hands."

"Of course not. That's my signature look."

Toni loved the tiny fake diamonds that she had embedded in the tips of all of her nails. She'd been doing it for years. It was part of her brand. She had diamonds on everything from her sunglasses to her handbags to her shoes.

Of course, very few of them were real diamonds, but one of the ways Lady Bianca rewarded her top sales people was with diamond jewelry, and she'd managed to win enough bling that her fingers sparkled in a gratifying way.

"And no snowflakes or reindeer or anything embarrassing."

"Honey. It's your manicure. You can have anything you want."

"Black? All I want is black."

Toni tried to be the kind of mother who never got into fights with her kid over stupid things. But there were limits to her patience. "No, not black. A color!"

Tiffany heaved a long sigh as though she had been asked to plow the family turnip field with her bare hands. "Fine."

In fact, they ended up having a lot of fun. She always liked to get her sales associates small gifts for the holiday season and being in a busy mall with Christmas carols playing and everybody bustling around buying each other presents made her happy. She even managed to strike up conversations with about half a dozen women and pass out her free makeover cards before Tiffany told her that if she did that one more time she would leave the mall and get the bus home. Since Toni knew her daughter was perfectly capable of doing just that, she tucked her cards away. "I can't help it. Something your grandmother said really got me excited again. You know, she's loving this positive thinking and I really think it's making a difference to her business."

While Toni had her broken nail repaired properly, Tiffany condescended to have a manicure. Toni realized she'd been conned when her daughter chose a pretty Christmas red for her nails and chatted away to the manicurist all during the procedure.

With their fresh, smooth nails and pampered hands, mother and daughter treated themselves to lunch out before heading home to get ready for the party. Tiffany wore a blue dress and heels without being begged. While she refused to let her mother do her makeup, she did at least improve on her usual routine of a swipe of lip-gloss. When she came out of her bedroom, Toni could see that she had applied eyeliner and blue eye shadow that brought out the pretty color in her eyes. Her lipstick was a muted pink. She might pretend to have zero interest in makeup but she'd either been listening to her mother or she'd picked up one of the Lady Bianca instruction cards on how to apply cosmetics. Naturally, Toni didn't mention any of this, she merely said, "You look so pretty, honey."

"Thanks, Mom. So do you."

Toni had chosen a red cocktail dress, which she wore with matching red heels that had just a delicate spray of diamonds across the toe.

The party was to start at four, but Toni and Tiffany had decided to arrive at three in order to help Linda with any last-minute details.

When they arrived, a strange van was parked in the driveway. Katie's Catering lettered the side so Toni's mild fear that the caterer might flake on them disappeared.

Even though it was still full daylight, Linda had all the lights on and it was quite a show. From the nativity scene still thankfully attached to the roof, to the icicles blinking on and off as they played *Here Comes Santa Claus* to the snowmen and reindeer in the front yard, every bit of decoration lit up.

Mrs. Schwartz might have cornered the gigantic Christmas sweater market, but Linda was holding her own in the over-the-top lighting department.

Tiffany stared from one house to the other and shook her head. "Have these people not heard of global warming?"

Linda opened the door before they could open it themselves. She was a sight to behold. She wore a blue satin dress exactly the color of the sapphires in her necklace, high-heeled silver shoes even more sparkly than Toni's and she'd piled her hair on top of her head. Naturally, she'd also done her makeup using the Holiday Glitter Palette from Lady Bianca.

"Mama, you look as glamorous as a movie star."

"Why, thank you, sweetheart. And don't you both look pretty enough to eat?"

Toni stepped into the house and smelled delicious scents coming from the oven. Two women bustled about, one setting up the bar and the other at the oven. Linda patted the one by the oven said, "Girls, this is Katie. We had the best time at her place the other night. Her friends all bought Lady Bianca products and Katie's very interested in becoming a sales consultant for us."

Katie was in her thirties, with dark hair pulled into a ponytail. She had soft, pretty features and wore square eyeglasses with red frames. Toni could tell that she'd used the glitter pack to do her makeup today. It seemed like a good omen. She wore a red apron that said Katie's Catering over a black blouse and slacks, and sent them a big smile when Linda introduced them both. "And that's my assistant, Theresa. She's also my little sister."

Theresa looked to be about Tiffany's age and blushed

with shyness when she was introduced. Tiffany walked over and asked if she could help and was soon chatting to her new acquaintance while she helped set up glasses and sliced lemons and limes.

Toni sent her mom a thumbs-up. Katie looked like she'd be a definite asset to the Lady Bianca team.

Katie was putting tiny sausage rolls on a large Christmas platter. Dolly Parton was singing about the holidays on the sound system, and every inch of the mobile home glistened, sparkled, twinkled or glowed.

There wasn't much to do with the catering staff but she and Tiff kept busy getting the furniture out of the way and putting some of the more breakable ornaments in cupboards.

"How many people are you expecting, Mama?"

Linda shrugged, looking vague. "There were about fifty on my e-vite list but not all of them will come. I hand-delivered invitations to all the residents of Pecan Heights, of course, and there were people at the parties I've been giving who I thought might enjoy coming."

Tiffany stared at her. "So, basically, you have no idea how many people are coming today?"

"No. Isn't it exciting?"

The weather wasn't warm but it was fair enough that people could congregate outside if they needed to if they could find room among all the lit-up Christmas decorations.

Soon Linda's guests began to arrive. The Schwartzes from across the street arrived first. Mrs. Schwartz had hand-knit a jolly-looking Santa to hang on the Christmas tree. Linda was delighted with it and removed one of the Lady Bianca glitter packs from the tree and replaced it with the Santa and then handed the glitter pack to Mrs. Schwartz. "I know you always say you don't want to host a Lady Bianca cosmetics party but wait until you see these colors. Or, if you just want a nice treat for yourself, you can have a Christmas makeover and you know it's complimentary."

As her guests continued to arrive, Linda received small gifts of jam and chocolates, homemade brownies and pralines. In turn, she pressed on each of her guests a Lady Bianca Christmas glitter pack, each containing a card offering the recipient a free makeover. Soon the sounds of chatter and merriment drowned out the country Christmas music.

Linda loved parties and her eyes glowed like the sapphires around her neck as she mingled among her guests, often stopping to introduce her daughter and granddaughter to people they didn't already know. The miserable woman from next door arrived, with her daughter in tow in spite of the fact that the daughter had not been invited. In honor of the season, Esther Kilpatrick wore a green velour jogging suit. Her green velour-covered behind was so massive that when she turned it looked like a putting green.

Linda, gracious as always, gave her unwelcome guests the glitter packs. "It's so nice to see you, Esther. And it's Cindy, isn't it?" she asked the daughter who was growing to look more like her mother every day.

When Linda turned to greet her next guests, Esther made an expression of disgust before tossing the glitter pack into her capacious bag. Her daughter ran her gaze greedily around the mobile home as though imagining her own furniture inside and her own curtains on the windows. Toni tried to think well of everybody but it was hard to like these two. It didn't seem like anyone else in the mobile home much cared for them either, so they stood in a corner drinking eggnog and talking to each other.

Linda squealed with excitement when a balding man with a big belly and a big smile arrived and pulled her into a hearty embrace. He wore designer jeans and a buttery soft leather jacket. With him was a tall man in his fifties with silver hair and a well-trimmed mustache who wore a gray suit and shiny loafers. Linda grabbed Toni's hand and pulled her forward. "I'm so happy to see you both. Toni's my daughter, I've told you all about her, and this is William Young and Henry Castillo. They're both in my success circle. William's a very wealthy real estate investor and Henry is an extremely successful lawyer. Toni is the top sales director for Lady Bianca in all of Texas and one of the top salespeople in the country," her mother said proudly.

Henry Castillo shook her hand politely, but William Young pulled her into a bear hug. He said, with a twinkle in his blue eyes, "I think you'd better watch out, young lady. The way your mother is going, she'll be taking that number one spot right from under your pretty feet."

They all laughed, but she could see how proud her mother was to be part of a group of successful people. It hadn't been easy, but she and Linda had come a long way from the trailer park where she'd grown up.

Linda loved people and she never worried whether they were rich or poor, important or nobody. Toni watched as Jim Tucker, the handyman, chatted with the wealthy real estate investor, as Linda had termed him, in the corner. As she walked by, it sounded like they were talking about termites.

Linda's clients ranged from her hairdresser to rich housewives to a budding country and western singer. They mingled with the mostly senior residents of Pecan Heights and munched coconut shrimp and pork sliders while sipping margaritas or glasses of wine.

The success circle's jeweler, Bert Green, arrived wearing a cowboy hat and a gorgeous pair of snakeskin boots with well-worn jeans and a denim shirt with a bolo tie. He wore his brown hair a little on the shaggy side and when he shook Toni's hand, she noticed several rings studded with some pretty impressive stones.

When Linda greeted him, he gave her a broad smile that showed even white teeth. "I've never seen one of my jewelry pieces look so perfect on anybody."

Linda's fingers fluttered up to touch the sapphire and diamond necklace. "Well, get used to it, you'll be seeing it around my neck quite a lot in the future."

He chuckled. "I believe it with all my heart," he said.

When Linda stepped away to greet more guests, Toni said, "I guess you'll be taking that necklace back home with you when you leave." She felt nervous every second that expensive piece of jewelry was hanging around her mother's neck. But he didn't seem to share her concern.

"Oh, there's no hurry. She can keep it for a few more days if she wants to."

"I'll just feel so much better when that jewelry is safely locked away."

He stared at her in surprise. "Toni, you can't think negative thoughts or you'll bring negative consequences." He patted her shoulder. "Remember: what you think, you manifest."

The mobile home was bursting at the seams with laughing, chatting people who didn't seem to mind that they had about as much personal space as passengers at rush hour on the New York subway. Toni walked over to rescue Tiffany from an older man who'd had too much to drink and seemed to be getting a little too affectionate. "Mr. Beasley. How are your grandchildren?" she asked in a loud voice.

"A real disappointment," he bellowed back. "Not like your pretty little girl here."

"I need to borrow Tiffany for a second so she can help in the kitchen," she said.

"Thanks, Mom," her daughter said. "I've never been hit on by anyone that old before. I didn't know what to do."

She was trying to think of a good answer when suddenly all the lights went out.

The living room was plunged not into pitch darkness but into a kind of dusk. With the sudden glitter of thousands and thousands of twinkling lights gone, her eyes were so dazzled that it took a moment for them to clear. In that moment, when conversation suddenly stopped, she heard the awful sound of a choking scream. She knew that voice.

"Mama? Mama!" She rushed forward, pushing people out of her way to the source of that scream. The lights went back on as suddenly as they'd gone off. She found her mother pale and wide-eyed, her hand against her throat.

The necklace was gone.

CHAPTER 5

*I*n seconds the cry of, "The necklace is gone!" made its way through the crowded room and outside to where some of the guests had gone for a breath of fresh air or a cigarette. In the general chaos, one voice boomed out. It was the lawyer, Henry Castillo. His presence was commanding, his voice booming. He stepped into the center of the room and said, "Nobody leaves!"

"Mama, what happened?"

Linda blinked at her in shock. "I honestly don't know. I was standing talking to Cheryl, you remember Cheryl, don't you? She's my hairdresser and one of my best clients. We were talking about hair extensions. When the lights went out, I felt the tiniest tickle, hardly anything at all, and when I put a hand to my chest the necklace was gone!" Her voice was rising.

Toni hastened to calm her down. "It's okay, Mama. We'll find it. Were you standing exactly here?"

"Yes, I think so."

Linda was standing near the wall, halfway between the

impromptu bar and the electric fireplace, now merrily flashing fake flames again with the power back on.

Cheryl, whose long blond hair probably owed a lot of its fullness to hair extensions, glanced down at the floor.

"Maybe the catch was faulty and the necklace slipped to the ground?"

She dropped to her knees and several other guests followed suit until half a dozen people crawled on the floor searching for a heap of glittery stones.

Meanwhile, a frozen sense of shock seemed to have afflicted the guests at Toni's mother's party. They were so quiet she could actually hear the plaintive melody of a country and western Christmas song. Somebody was begging their daddy not to get drunk this Christmas.

Then the shock began to wear off. She heard voices. One said, "I don't understand, what happened?"

This voice was answered by another voice. "Linda lost her necklace. It's worth like a million bucks."

"Not a million," another voice chimed in. "More like a hundred grand."

"Well, she lost it!"

Suddenly, Linda spoke in a clear, loud voice. "I did not lose that necklace. Somebody stole it."

The jeweler stood in the middle of the room looking as stunned as Linda. Rapidly, Toni tried to re-create the scene as she had witnessed it moments before the lights went out. She headed back to Tiffany, who not only had youthful eyes but a fantastic visual memory. She took her daughter's arm. "Who was standing near Grandma right before the lights went out?"

Tiffany closed her eyes and Toni could see her pulling the

scene into her mind the way she'd pull a computer file up on her desktop.

Bert Green said in a firm tone, "I'm sorry to do this, but everybody's going to have to empty their pockets, purses, briefcases, shopping bags. Every person here will have to be searched before they head out." Now that his initial shock had worn off, he seemed like a man accustomed to command.

"Excellent plan, Bert," Henry Castillo said.

"But that's ridiculous!" The complaining voice rose. Toni recognized it as belonging to Esther Kilpatrick, the next-door neighbor. "You can't treat us like a bunch of common criminals. I came here for a nice visit with my neighbors. I am not going to be searched." She was red in the face and seemed even bigger in her anger. As she headed for the sliding door, the jeweler stepped in front of her. "I'm sorry, ma'am. We can search you now, and I'm sure we can get a couple of ladies to volunteer to help. Or, you can wait for the police to get here."

"Tiffany?"

Her daughter tried to ignore the confusion and focus. "I turned away from Mr. Beasley. Ugh. And looked over toward the kitchen." She blew out a breath. "I don't know, Mom. It was so crowded."

"Did you see Grandma?"

"I could see her hair and a bit of her dress. She was talking to Cheryl, her hairdresser. I could see Cheryl's back."

"Think about it. Who was behind Grandma?"

"A bunch of people."

"Okay, let's try this. Where was Bert Green, the jeweler in the cowboy hat?"

Tiff closed her eyes. "Cowboy hat. Over by the window. Beside a woman I didn't know."

"Jim Tucker? He's tall, did you see him?"

Tiffany's eyes were still closed. She took a moment. "No. I didn't see him."

"What about the rest of the success circle? Where were they?"

"I saw the investor guy go out with a cigar a couple minutes ago. I think the lawyer was at the bar getting a drink. Katie's too short. I couldn't see her at all."

The whole time she and Tiffany had been talking, Esther Kilpatrick and Bert Green had continued their argument. Esther sputtered with annoyance. "Just because that no good tramp chose to wear a priceless necklace to a Christmas party in a trailer park, you expect me to subject myself to a strip search?"

"Somebody call the cops," Bert said, his voice rising too.

At that moment, Luke Marciano stepped in through the sliding doors. His cop's gaze rapidly scanned the crowd and then he walked forward to where Toni was standing. "Did I just hear somebody say call the cops?" he asked.

"Luke, I have never been so glad to see you in all my life. Linda just got robbed. Somebody knocked out the power for a couple of minutes and stole that necklace right off her neck."

He nodded grimly. "I should have got here earlier."

Just then, she saw a sudden movement through the sliding door. Somebody was striding away from Linda's mobile home, from the direction of the kitchen door. Luke's gaze connected with hers briefly and without a word being spoken, he pushed back through the crowd and out into the night.

"Well, I've got nothing to hide," Mr. Beasley said. "Anybody can go ahead and search me. Just watch out for my colostomy bag."

"Lord have mercy," Toni murmured under her breath.

Linda put her arms around Tiffany. "One minute that necklace was on my neck, and the next minute it was just gone."

Tiffany patted her back. "Try not to get too upset, Grandma. We'll figure this out."

"All I wanted to do was manifest success, and I think I've manifested disaster."

By this time, Luke had his man. He dragged Jim Tucker, the handyman, back through the door. The man looked both defiant and sheepish. "What the hell? I was heading home to get my supper."

Luke glanced at Toni. "You know this guy?"

In the background Christmas music played. Henry Young, who'd come in behind Luke, said, "Can somebody turn the music off?"

Theresa, the caterer's sister, found the music dock and switched off the music. It was suddenly amazingly silent in the room considering there must have been sixty people crammed in there. Toni answered Luke's question. "Yes. I know this man. He's Jim Tucker. He's the resident caretaker. Why would you run away, Jim?"

"I didn't run anywhere, I told you, I was going home to get some supper." She was good at reading people and while his words sounded plausible, he shifted and wouldn't meet her gaze.

"My mother just had an expensive piece of jewelry stolen. You left from the kitchen door, and in a big hurry. The main breaker is in the utility room behind the kitchen, but you know that. You've been in here a hundred times doing chores and fixing things. You could have knocked the power out and put it back on easily."

He raised his head and glared at her. "I didn't steal nothin'. Go ahead and search me."

Luke could be intimidating when he wanted to and he turned so he was right in Jim's face. "I think I prefer to interrogate you at the police station. We've got all our resources and records there. We can see what kind of background you have. If you've ever been arrested before. Any secrets you have, I'll know them within a couple of hours."

Jim Tucker's face grew dark red and his gaze dropped to the ground. She knew Luke had only been fishing, but it looked like he'd caught something. Jim Tucker glared then dropped his gaze once more. "It was just a prank. Knocking out the power. Stupid prank."

Luke asked, "Who hired you?"

"A guy in the bar. Gave me a hundred bucks to do it. It was a Christmas prank. He said it would be funny to see the best lit house in the park go dark right in the middle of her party."

Linda was vibrating with fury. "Jim Tucker. I have always trusted you. I let you wash my windows, inside as well as out, and this is the thanks I get? I've always given you a nice tip for Christmas and remembered your birthday."

The man kept his gaze stubbornly on the floor. "Like I said, I thought it was just a prank."

Luke continued in that same maddeningly calm voice. Toni knew his interrogating voice well, from when they first met, when she had been the suspect in a murder case. He could be very unnerving. "This guy who hired you, is he here today?"

Jim Tucker shook his head.

"Pick your head up and have a good look at everybody here. Let's make absolutely sure. If I find you lied to me, there's going to be trouble."

Jim Tucker did as he was told and gazed around the room. Then he shook his head. "Guy's not here."

"Which bar was it?"

He named a seedy bar a couple of miles down the road.

"What did this person who hired you look like?"

Jim shrugged. "It was pretty dark. I'd had a couple beers. He was maybe forty-something. Big fella in a plaid shirt. Smelled like sweat."

"How tall?"

Another shrug. "Shorter than me."

"Hair color? Eye color?"

Like I said, it was dark. I don't know. Maybe dark hair."

Toni spoke. "Did the guy tell you what time to cut the power?"

"Yeah. At five-thirty, exactly."

Because an open house that went from four until eight was going to be at its most crowded right in the middle hours.

"I think I know who hired Jim."

She was suddenly and completely the center of attention as though a spotlight had been shone on her. She squeezed her mom's shoulder in support and stepped forward. "Esther? Do you happen to have a photograph of your son-in-law?"

The woman's jaw dropped and her face turned red with fury. "My son-in-law? How dare you?"

"You don't want a picture of him," Mr. Schwartz said. "He's a hooligan. Everybody says so."

She turned to Cindy, Esther's daughter. "You've been

sizing up this place since you got here like you were measuring for curtains. Do you have a picture of your husband that you could show Jim Tucker?"

She spluttered like her mother and echoed, "How dare you?"

Esther Kilpatrick, her arms quivering with rage, suddenly grabbed her purse, pushed the Christmas goodies off the serving table so a chafing dish and two trays tumbled to the floor, shortbread cookies and Swedish meatballs bouncing and jumbling, and turned her capacious bag upside down and shook it. Out of her bag fell her wallet, breath mints, eyeglasses, three of Linda's glitter packs, a cellphone, a couple of bingo chips and so much spare change that it sounded like she'd just won on a slot machine. She pointed dramatically to the pile. "There. Go through my things." She threw her arms in the air with great drama. "Search me. You won't find a diamond and sapphire necklace."

"No. I know I won't," Toni continued.

She turned to Bert Green, the jeweler. "I'm guessing all your jewelry's insured. Isn't it?"

He nodded. "Of course it is. I've had two break-ins in my career. Be stupid not to have insurance."

"So, if this necklace disappears, you could just put in a claim."

It was his turn to glare at her with anger. "Are you suggesting I stole my own necklace? Why would I do that? Your mom's a nice lady. And I want her to succeed in her life and her business."

"So, if you think so highly of my mother, and you were already insured, why did you need to put a lien on her mobile home?"

He pulled his hat off and put it on again. "If I make another claim, I won't be able to afford the insurance premiums anymore."

"You weren't going to lend my mother this necklace, were you?"

He shook his head. "Sorry, Linda. It was never personal."

Linda looked completely confused and smaller somehow without the necklace. She asked, "Did you steal the necklace so you could claim the insurance?" The betrayal in her eyes was heartrending.

Bert stepped forward and put his hands out. "No. I would never do that."

Toni spoke up, "No, you didn't. You passed on the risk to one of your good friends in the success circle."

She turned to the lawyer who was standing beside the tree with his hands in his pockets. He nodded. "That's right," he said. "We all believe in Linda." He smiled at her as though he were a beloved uncle. "When Bert couldn't bring himself to lend her the necklace, I said I'd take on the risk."

"So, if the necklace doesn't turn up, you're legally entitled to this mobile home."

He made a sound of derision. "Young lady, I own an executive five-bedroom house. What would I want with a mobile home?" He glanced around at the assembled party guests, many of whom lived in similar mobile homes. "No offense intended."

"You don't want the home. Esther Kilpatrick does. She tried to get Linda out of here twice. First, she claimed Linda was contravening the bylaws by running a business out of her home. But that didn't fly." She turned to the woman. "You want your daughter living next door to you. And you want your son-in-law close so you can keep an eye on him. But the problem is, Linda had no intention of moving. You had to find a way to force her out."

"This is the most ridiculous thing I've ever heard. I am leaving." The woman began angrily to shove her belongings back into her bag. When she turned to leave, she found that Luke was blocking her path.

He said, "I don't think so. Let's hear what Toni has to say."

"This is police brutality. If you don't get out of my way, I'll sue you," she jabbed a blunt fingertip at him, "sue the police department, and I'll sue Pecan Heights Mobile Home Park."

Toni said, "You like suing people, don't you? You've been doing it for years. I knew I'd seen the lawyer before but I couldn't place him. He got out of your car at the hospital parking lot. Your car is very recognizable." She turned to Luke, whose hobby was restoring old cars and trucks. "It's a 1970 Plymouth Roadrunner."

"Nice," he said.

"I only caught a glimpse of Henry Castillo, getting out of your car, but I'd be willing to bet that if we did some digging, we'd find out that he's the lawyer who's been taking on all your bogus lawsuits."

"I don't know where you dreamed all this up," Henry Castillo said. He drew himself up to his full height, which was impressive. "Why would I take part in an underhanded scheme to snatch a mobile home?"

"Is this woman a client of yours?" Luke asked.

He rocked back and forth on his heels as though he were getting ready to address a judge. "There is such a thing as attorney-client privilege. Whether this woman is a client of mine or not—and I have so many clients I cannot keep track of them all—is immaterial. It is inconceivable that a man of my stature in the community would belittle himself to steal a mobile home—and from a member of my own success circle."

There was silence and then of all people, the next one to speak was Tiffany. She said, "I was at the hospital that day. For the children's party. I saw you perform." She turned to Toni. "I knew I'd seen him before, too, but he wore a costume and makeup. I didn't make the connection until you said you'd seen him at the hospital. It was when you were picking me up after the party, right?"

"That's right."

Henry Castillo gazed down at Tiffany as though she were stupid, which made Toni's blood start to boil. She was used to people thinking she wasn't very bright, but nobody treated her daughter that way. He said, "I'm not a performer. If you'd been listening, you'd know I'm a lawyer."

"You're also an amateur magician."

Linda spoke for the first time. "That's right, he is an amateur magician. Everyone in my success circle volunteers. It's our way of giving back. Why would you lie about that, Henry?"

"This is ridiculous," he said.

Tiffany spoke to Luke. "I was volunteering at the hospital; I do it to get extra credit for my college applications. I was helping at the holiday party for the sick kids and as part of the entertainment, he did a magic show."

Her tone changed, hardened. She spoke directly to Henry Castillo. "You were really good. So light-fingered. You kept making things disappear and reappear." She glanced around. "The kids loved it."

He nodded. "Thank you for speaking up in my defense. As you can see, I'm a pillar of the community. Hardly a petty thief."

Toni glanced at Tiffany and winked. "I don't think she was speaking in your defense. I think she was pointing out that you have lots of practice making things disappear."

CHAPTER 6

"Ms. Diamond, there's quite a difference between causing a paper flower to appear behind a young girl's ear or finding a coin mysteriously behind a young boy's kneecap and spiriting away a valuable necklace."

She caught Luke watching her and could tell he was enjoying himself. They shared an intimate glance before she turned back to the lawyer, currently on trial for his reputation. "I think it's exactly the same. It's all sleight-of-hand. A man who can do those kinds of tricks could probably have the clasp undone and the necklace off my mother's neck in moments."

"Again, I must ask what you think my motive could be?"

"Let me ask you a question, sir. Why are you in the success circle? If your business is doing so well, why do you need positive thinking? Why would you ever work for a client like Esther Kilpatrick? I'm guessing you're not as successful as you try to appear. It's expensive keeping up a five-bedroom executive home and a fancy lifestyle.

"Maybe Esther Kilpatrick had something on you or maybe you just needed the money. But, if that necklace disappears, and you get my mother's mobile home, you'll sell it to Esther and her daughter. And, you'll also end up with a nice necklace. Also worth a lot of money."

"You're too stupid for words. Have you forgotten that I took on the risk of that necklace? I'm the one who has to pay Bert Green if it goes missing."

"I'm perfectly aware of that. You'll give him what he paid. Which is the wholesale price." She turned to the jeweler. "Am I right?"

"You are."

"I'm guessing a guy like you has contacts, maybe a fence. I bet you'll still come out ahead on the deal. Maybe you'll have it broken up into the stones and made into a gift for your wife."

"That's ridiculous."

"Is it?"

He held his arms out wide. "I hate to be dramatic, but go ahead and search me. If you think I stole that necklace, you go ahead and find it."

She said, "Oh, I know exactly where it is."

A murmur arose in the room. All eyes turned to her. She exchanged a glance with Luke and he nodded and stepped a little closer to the lawyer.

She walked over to the fireplace. She said, "As every good magician knows, always hide things in plain sight." She turned to the Latina Madonna who smiled down at her from the mantel. She reached around the neck and among the layers of sparkly jewels she picked up the sapphire and diamond necklace.

"You were standing by the drink table when the lights went out. Exactly at the moment you'd paid Jim Tucker to cut the power. You were two steps behind my mother. All you had to do was slip behind her and remove the necklace. In the surprise of the power outage, everyone was startled. You had all the time you needed to slip it off and slip it over the Madonna's head. By the time the lights came back on, you were on the other side of the room standing by the Christmas tree."

She handed the necklace to her mother but Linda put her hands up as though warding away an evil spirit. "No. I don't want it."

Relieved to the bottom of her shoes, Toni turned to Bert Green and passed him the necklace. "I'm giving this back to you. Please go and put it in a safe somewhere."

He accepted the jewelry but with an apologetic shrug pulled out a jeweler's loupe. "I hope you don't mind, but with all the shenanigans, I need to make sure this is the right necklace." He fitted the loupe to his eye. He took a moment to study the stones and then nodded, satisfied. "This is my necklace. Linda, I'm sorry it turned out this way. Please believe me, I had nothing to do with stealing your necklace." He smiled at her. "And it is yours. Believe in it."

"Thanks, Bert." But she didn't look convinced.

"WELL," Bert said. Then he didn't seem quite sure how to finish the sentence, so he said, "Well," again and then finally, "It's been a real interesting evening." His gaze hardened as he turned to the lawyer, and he said, "Henry, I don't suppose we'll be seeing you back at the Circle of Success."

William Young shook his head. "Absolutely not. Consider yourself fired, Henry."

Bert said, "I've got another lawyer in mind who I think would be a better fit with our group." He walked over to Linda and to everyone's surprise, pulled her in for a hug. "Linda, you are exactly the kind of person we want in our success circle. You're positive, hard-working, and I know you're going to be a very successful woman. Don't let a little hiccup like this throw you off your stride." He raised his head, nodded generally to everyone and headed out the door, the diamond and sapphire necklace clutched tightly in his hand.

William, the wealthy investor, followed him. "Bert, I'll grab a ride with you, if you don't mind. I came with Henry."

With a wave and a quick, "Thanks," he rushed out the door after his friend.

Luke walked over to Linda. He said, "Linda, you throw a hell of a party. I think I'll take Henry Castillo, and your neighbor Esther and Jim the handyman down to the station. We'll get all the pieces of this crazy plot put together."

The lawyer blustered, "You can't arrest me. You've got no proof."

Luke glanced at him in surprise. "Who said anything about arrest? I'm taking you down to the station for questioning. On suspicion of, well, I've got a few suspicions. We'll talk about them when we get downtown."

Suddenly, Esther, whose complexion had been fluctuating between icy white and bright red, banged her fist against the wall so that the icicles outside waved and shimmered and

Here Comes Santa Claus missed a beat. Her face was diffused with red as she turned to Henry Castillo and yelled, "You had to be so fancy. I told you I was going to get Charlie to bang her over the head and steal the necklace. You had to be Mr. Clever-Fingers and show off that you can slide a necklace off a lady's neck without her even noticing. Last time I ever listen to you. You're just like my ex-husband. You're a loser."

Henry Castillo's face grew gray and his voice was icy as he said, "Shut up, Esther."

"Or what? They got nothing on me. All I want is to buy this house for my daughter and my son-in-law. There's no crime against that. You're the one that got all fancy playing your tricks, stealing jewelry in broad daylight. You're an idiot. And you're fired. I'll be finding myself a new lawyer. In fact, I'm going to find a lawyer to sue your ass."

"You think the detective here isn't going to be interested in some of the stories I know about you? And your precious son-in-law?"

"You gotta love the holiday spirit," Luke said, sounding as cheerful as though he had just been handed a Christmas present, which, come to think of it, he had. He looked around. "How many witnesses heard that exchange and would be willing to go on record?"

Two dozen hands went up. "Okay, folks. I appreciate your community spirit. Toni, I'll see you later." He leaned over and gave her a big smacking kiss on the mouth. He so rarely showed her affection in front of other people that she took a moment before smiling and kissing him back. He leaned in and said in a low voice, "My life is never dull when you three women are around."

"Are you complaining?"

He chuckled softly. "Not even for a second." He ran his hand down her back. "By the way, you look hot. I'll call you later."

As Luke left with the still protesting lawyer and the furious neighbor, as well as the silent handyman, the party suddenly hit that moment when staying would be an anticlimax. There was a flurry of exclamations: "Linda, are you okay?" And, "I think we should get the board together to see if we can get rid of Esther Kilpatrick. We don't want her in our park."

Mr. Schwartz looked around and said, "And I don't know about you people, but I'm thinking we need to hire a new handyman, too."

Mr. Beasley kissed Linda on the cheek. "I never had so much fun at a Christmas party in all my life."

Linda, who was beginning to get her color back, said brightly, "And, look on the bright side. You're all entitled to a free makeover. There's me, my daughter Toni, and we've got plenty of wonderful Lady Bianca Associates who would be more than happy to come on over and make sure every lady in this park and every daughter, sister, cousin, and friend is looking her absolute best for the holidays."

"I think it would be good for my knitting club to have makeovers," Mrs. Schwartz suddenly announced. "It would do us all good. You're a wonderful neighbor, Linda. Don't ever change."

When the caterers had packed up and gone, and only Linda, Toni, and Tiffany were left, crashed out on the couch, munching leftover shortbread, Toni said, "Mama, that was brilliant catching them all just at that moment. Even Mrs. Schwartz finally cracked. I think we can be doing makeovers and parties nonstop through the end of the year."

Linda smiled and touched her neck as though her necklace were still there. Her eyes dimmed for a moment before her natural cheerfulness reasserted itself. "I realized that since everybody in Pecan Heights has become so competitive with the Christmas decorations, that I should encourage that same spirit with personal appearance. Can you imagine if every woman in Pecan Heights tried to look prettier than her neighbors? I'll be swimming in diamonds."

Tiffany nibbled the head off a shortbread snowman. "Are you going to keep going to that Circle of Success, Grandma? Now the guy turned out to be a crook?"

Linda patted her bare neck once more, as though it were a favorite pet. "I don't know, honey. I was so sure that if I believed in diamonds and really focused on them that they would appear in my life. Maybe I was fooling myself."

Toni thought this might be the moment to tell Linda that all her hard work and her confident belief in herself over the past months had, in fact, pushed her sales at a level that she'd won her choice of diamond earrings or a modest diamond ring. "Mama," she began. She stopped when a soft knock sounded on the patio door.

They all looked at each other.

"Maybe it's Luke come back," Linda said.

Toni shook her head. "He'll be interviewing those guys at the station for quite a while. Anyway, I don't think he'd knock."

"Well, I hope it's not another partygoer. All the food and drinks have been packed away and I don't have any more party spirit in me." Linda rose and went to the door and when she opened it, she made a funny sound like a squawk. Then she cried, "Roy!"

Roy?

She and Tiffany stared at each other. Tiffany said, "Really? Grandma's boyfriend from the cruise? *That* Roy?"

They waited in suspense, but sure enough, it was Roy from the cruise. He and Linda had met over bingo in the Caribbean.

He blushed when he saw them all. "I'm sorry I'm late for your party. My plane was delayed. I was hoping to surprise you."

"Oh, Roy, you did surprise me. Did you fly all the way from Omaha? For my little Christmas party?"

He looked a little bashful. "That, and I wanted to see you again."

There was a flutter of romance in the air, and it was exactly what Linda needed to take her mind off the unfortunate incident of the Christmas party. Toni grabbed Tiffany's hand and said, "We should go."

"No," Roy said. "Please don't."

Linda said, "Let's all sit down." She and Roy sat side-by-side on the couch and he took her hand.

"I was struggling a little in my business. At first, I emailed Linda because I had enjoyed her company so much on the boat. I thought we could maintain a friendship. Then she started talking to me about these books she was reading on positive thinking and how you can change your reality by changing your thoughts, and I began to see that she was right. When I started implementing some of her ideas, I noticed changes. Well, I don't want to boast, but I got the biggest Christmas bonus I've ever had this year. And I was worried I was going to lose my job. Anyway, I had to come and see you again, Linda."

"I am so happy all that positive thinking worked for you. I'm not so sure it worked for me."

He shook his head. "If you start talking negative to me, I'm going to have to repeat some of those excellent pieces of advice you gave me."

He blushed deeper, and then he reached into his coat pocket and pulled out a small box wrapped in Christmas paper and tied with a gold bow. "Merry Christmas, Linda."

"Oh, Roy, you shouldn't have got me a present."

"Honestly, you changed my life. And I wanted to show my appreciation for how special you are."

Linda looked delighted as she pulled off the bow and tore off the wrapping. Under the wrapping was a jewelry box. "Oh my gosh." She opened the box and let out a cry of joy. Then she eased out the necklace. It consisted of a delicate gold chain and suspended from the chain was a small sapphire surrounded by tiny diamonds so the piece resembled a flower.

Roy looked thrilled at her response. "I can't believe that necklace is exactly the right color for your dress," he said.

Linda laughed shakily. "Would you be kind enough to put it on for me?"

Toni and Tiffany watched as Roy carefully fastened the delicate necklace around Linda's neck.

She jumped up and checked out her reflection in the mirror. "It's perfect."

Her eyes were shining as she said, "You see, girls, positive thinking really does work. I believed I'd have a diamond necklace for Christmas, and here it is."

She threw her arms around Roy and hugged him. "You don't know what this means to me. Thank you."

Toni and Tiffany stood as one. Toni said, "I hope we'll be seeing more of you, Roy?"

"You sure will. If it's okay with your mama, I thought I'd stay for the holidays."

Linda touched the necklace the way she'd been touching the much larger one earlier. "We'd be delighted if you joined us for Christmas."

As they walked out the front door and headed for their car, Tiffany said, "Do you think he's kissing her right now?"

"I don't know. Would it be rude to peek?"

"Yeah, totally rude."

They both turned and looked back. Through the window they saw Linda wrapped in Roy's arms.

As they got in the car, Tiffany said, "So, this positive thinking thing. Maybe it works after all."

"I think if we've learned anything, it's that sometimes what you think you want brings something entirely different, but so much better."

"You know what, Mom?"

"What?"

"I have a positive feeling that we're going to have a good Christmas this year."

A Note from Nancy

Dear Reader,

Thank you for reading *A Diamond Choker for Christmas*. I am so grateful for all the enthusiasm the *Toni Diamond Mysteries* has received.

I hope you'll consider leaving a review and please tell your friends who like cozy mysteries.

Review on Amazon, Goodreads or BookBub.

Don't let the fun end. Let's stay in touch.

Join my newsletter to hear about my new releases and enjoy prizes and bonus content like the Vampire Knitting Club's free prequel, *Tangles and Treasons*, the exciting tale of how the gorgeous Rafe Crosyer was turned into a vampire.

I hope to see you in my private Facebook Group Nancy Warren's Knitwits where the fun continues daily.

Until next time,
Happy Reading,

Nancy

ALSO BY NANCY WARREN

The best way to keep up with new releases, plus enjoy bonus content and prizes is to join Nancy's newsletter at NancyWarrenAuthor.com or join her in her private FaceBook group Nancy Warren's Knitwits.

~

Toni Diamond Mysteries

Toni Diamond is a successful saleswoman for Lady Bianca Cosmetics in this series of humorous cozy mysteries.

Frosted Shadow - Book 1

Ultimate Concealer - Book 2

Midnight Shimmer - Book 3

A Diamond Choker For Christmas - A Holiday Whodunnit

Toni Diamond Mysteries Boxed Set: Books 1-4

Vampire Knitting Club: Paranormal Cozy Mystery

Lucy Swift inherits an Oxford knitting shop and the late-night knitting club of vampires who live downstairs.

Tangles and Treason - A free ebook for newsletter subscribers. A paperback version is available for sale. NancyWarrenAuthor.com

The Vampire Knitting Club - Book 1

Stitches and Witches - Book 2

Crochet and Cauldrons - Book 3

Stockings and Spells - Book 4

LARGE PRINT EDITIONS: Vampire Knitting Club

Available in paperback or hardback large print format.

Vampire Knitting Club: Cornwall: Paranormal Cozy Mystery

Boston-bred witch Jennifer Cunningham agrees to run a knitting and yarn shop in a fishing village in Cornwall, England—with characters from the Oxford-set *Vampire Knitting Club* series.

Village Flower Shop: Paranormal Cozy Mystery

In a picture-perfect Cotswold village, flowers, witches, and murder make quite the bouquet for flower shop owner Peony Bellefleur.

Vampire Book Club: Paranormal Women's Fiction Cozy Mystery

Seattle witch Quinn Callahan's midlife crisis is interrupted when she gets sent to Ballydehag, Ireland, to run an unusual bookshop.

Great Witches Baking Show: Paranormal Culinary Cozy Mystery

Poppy Wilkinson, an American with English roots, joins a reality show to win the crown of Britain's Best Baker—and to get inside Broomewode Hall to uncover the secrets of her past.

The Great Witches Baking Show - Book 1

Baker's Coven - Book 2

A Rolling Scone - Book 3

A Bundt Instrument - Book 4

Blood, Sweat and Tiers - Book 5

Crumbs and Misdemeanors - Book 6

A Cream of Passion - Book 7

Cakes and Pains - Book 8

Whisk and Reward - Book 9

Gingerdead House - A Holiday Whodunnit

The Great Witches Baking Show Boxed Set: Books 1-3

The Great Witches Baking Show Boxed Set: Books 4-6 (includes bonus novella)

The Great Witches Baking Show Boxed Set: Books 7-9

Abigail Dixon: 1920s Cozy Historical Mystery

In 1920s Paris everything is très chic, except murder.

Murder at the Paris Fashion House - Book 1

Death at Darrington Manor - Book 2

The Almost Wives Club: Contemporary Romantic Comedy

An enchanted wedding dress is a matchmaker in this series of romantic comedies where five runaway brides find out who the best men really are.

The Almost Wives Club: Kate - Book 1

Take a Chance: Contemporary Romance

Meet the Chance family, a cobbled together family of eleven kids who are all grown up and finding their ways in life and love.

For a complete list of books, check out Nancy's website at NancyWarrenAuthor.com

ABOUT THE AUTHOR

Nancy Warren is the USA Today Bestselling author of more than 70 novels. She's originally from Vancouver, Canada, though she tends to wander and has lived in England, Italy and California at various times. Favorite moments include being the answer to a crossword puzzle clue in Canada's National Post newspaper, being featured on the front page of the New York Times when her book Speed Dating launched Harlequin's NASCAR series, and being nominated three times for Romance Writers of America's RITA award. She has an MA in Creative Writing from Bath Spa University. She's an avid hiker, loves chocolate and most of all, loves to hear from readers! The best way to stay in touch is to sign up for Nancy's newsletter at www.nancywarren.net.

To learn more about Nancy and her books
www.nancywarren.net